Park City
Past & Present™

Rick Pieros Photography

About the Author & Photographer

Rick Pieros has been traveling the rural and wild areas of the western United States since his youth. Drawn to the remnants of the American West's rich and colorful past, Rick switched from a path pursuing purely nature photography, to follow his passion of documenting the quickly vanishing artifacts of the western experience. Besides his Park City photographic work, Rick's current emphasis is on abstract details of weathered detritus; miner's shacks, abandoned automobiles, mining equipment, and other items left behind to be patinated by the elements.

Rick owned and operated Wild Spirits Nature Photography studio on historic Main Street in Park City, Utah until 2007. He currently lives at the base of the Wasatch Mountains with his wife Heidi, and two daughters Hailey and Ivy. To view Rick's portfolio of Park City images, or to order limited edition photographs, please visit www.RickPieros.com.

Additional information on *Park City - Past & Present* can be found by visiting www.ParkCityPastandPresent.com.

Copyright © 2011 Rick Pieros Photography. All rights reserved. This book may not be reproduced or quoted in whole or in part by any means whatsoever without the written permission by the publisher.

Publisher Information:
Rick Pieros
Rick Pieros Photography
P.O. Box 982181
Park City, Utah 84098

ISBN 978-1-4507-5915-1 softbound
ISBN 978-0-578-09440-3 hardbound

Front Cover Photograph: McPolin Farm, 2002.
Back Cover Photographs: Silver King Mill, 1935 & 2010.

Printed in China by Global PSD

Miner's Shack; Daly Canyon, 2003.

Acknowledgements

The journey of writing, photographing, and publishing *Park City - Past & Present* has been an extraordinary experience. There were many helping hands along the way. I would like to personally thank Sandra Morrison, Wendy Ashton, and Emily Beeson of the Park City Museum for their invaluable knowledge and assistance. I would also like to thank the Utah State Historical Society for their helpful research. All of the historic photographs in *Park City - Past & Present* are used by the permission of the Park City Museum, the Park City Museum, Pop Jenks Collection, and the Utah State Historical Society. All individual photography credits can be found at the end of the book.

Fellow Utah author and photographer Ann Torrence, offered many great publishing insights early on in the process. Ann's latest book, *US 89: the Scenic Route to Seven National Parks*, is a fantastic regional book and a must have. Corbet Curfman & Anna Katherine Curfman of Riverbed Design deserve a special thanks for their expertise and assistance in shepherding *Park City - Past & Present* through the design and publishing process. Most importantly, I would like to thank my wife Heidi. This book would have been impossible without her support and encouragement.

Sunrise over The Canyons Resort, St. Mary's Church, 2009.

McPolin Farm, The Canyons Resort in background, 2005.

Contents

A Sense of Place:
The Founding of Park City — 6

Park City: Boomtown to Ski Town — 7
- Ontario Mill — 8
- Daly West Mine — 10
- Marsac Mill — 12
- Silver King Consolidated Mill — 14
- California Comstock Mill — 15
- Silver King Coalition Mines Building — 16
- Silver King Mill — 18
- Daly Judge Mill — 20
- Judge Mine Assay Office — 22
- Judge Zinc Smelter — 24
- Park City Consolidated Mine — 26
- Spiro Machine Shop — 28

Architecture of Old Town:
If These Walls Could Talk — 30
- Main Street — 30
- Old Town View — 32
- Star Meat & Grocery — 34
- Windsor Billiards — 36
- Golden Rule Mercantile — 38
- First National Bank — 40
- The New York Cafe — 42
- China Bridge — 43
- Morrison Merrill & Co. — 44
- Kimball's Garage — 46
- The Line — 48
- New Park Hotel - Claimjumper — 49
- Park Motor - National Garage — 50

California - Comstock Mill, Park City Mountain Resort, 2006.

Park City Railroads	52
Union Pacific Railroad Depot	52
Denver & Rio Grande Railroad Depot	54
Crescent Railroad	56
Public Life & Buildings	58
Park City Fire Dept. & Old City Hall	58
Sheriff's Office & Park City Police Dept.	60
Washington School	62
Marsac School	63
Park City High School	64
U.S. Post Office	66
St. Mary's Church	68
Park City LDS Meeting House	69
Miners Hospital	70
Skiing in Park City: A Brief History	72
Ecker Hill - Utah Olympic Park	72
Nelson Farm - Park City Mountain Resort	74
Snow Park Resort - Deer Valley Resort	76
Park City West Resort - The Canyons	78
Early Life in the Snyderville Basin	80
Snyderville Basin View	80
McPolin Farm	82
Pop Jenks	84
Kimball Hotel & Ranch	85
Afterword: A Treasure to Keep?	86
Afterword: A Treasure to Keep?	86
Dedication - Glenwood Cemetery	87
Photography Credits & Notes	88
Photograph Credits	88
Photographer Notes	88

A Sense of Place: The Founding of Park City

What does it mean to have a "sense of place"? Is a "sense of place" the shared vision of community? Is it simply shared experience and interests? Is it the silent and reflective smiles on everyone's faces after a big powder day? The familiar welcome of the McPolin Farm as you drive into town? Could a "sense of place" in past eras have been the shared hardships of a less affluent populace? Like all good things, you know it in your bones, but are at a loss for words to explain it to one who doesn't understand from first hand experience. Park City has had many eras and several boom and bust cycles. Through it all a tight knit community and a "sense of place" has remained.

In 1847, Brigham Young and Mormon Pioneers passed just north of what is present day Park City on their way to settle the Salt Lake Valley. Later in 1862, the United States Government sent troops under the command of Colonel Patrick Conner to guard the U.S. mail and to keep an eye on the burgeoning Mormon enclave near the Great Salt Lake. Connor's troops established an Army outpost in the western foothills above Salt Lake City, that eventually became Fort Douglas. Believing that a gold or silver strike would attract outsiders to dilute the Mormon population, Colonel Conner sent soldiers out prospecting in the Wasatch Mountains. In the fall of 1868, prospecting Army soldiers discovered rich silver veins in the hills above what would become Park City. With a winter storm on the way, the soldiers marked the silver discovery with a stick and a bandana so they could find their strike next spring. The mine was eventually named Flagstaff, in reference to the bandana placed atop the stick, and became the first mine to ship ore from Park City.

George Snyder, a Mormon polygamist, built a boarding house in Old Town with his wife Rhoda to profit from the mining trade. According to local legend, George declared on the Fourth of July, 1872, "We shall call this place Parley's Park City." Soon thereafter, "Parley" (named for early Mormon settler Parley Pratt) was dropped and a boom town had its name. Park City was incorporated twelve years later in 1884.

One of the last surviving boarding house buildings in Old Town; Alaskan Boarding House, Main Street, 2009.

Welcome to Park City, State Highway 224.

Old Town Park City, circa 1891.

Utah Olympic Park, 2007.

Park City: Boomtown to Ski Town

After the discovery of the Flagstaff strike, other major mining discoveries were quick to occur. Among those discoveries were the Ontario Mine in 1872, the Daly West Mine in 1881, the Crescent, Anchor, and Mayflower Mines in 1882, and the Silver King Mine in 1894. Silver production boomed in Park City along with the population of miners, merchants, and other fortune seekers. In 1889 the population was 5,000, which was a great sight from the 164 souls that called Parley's Park home in 1870. Seven years later in 1896 the population was 7,000, which is close to Park City's current population of 8,000 people. Park City's population eventually topped out around 9,000 individuals in 1898, the year that the Great Fire destroyed three quarters of the town. The majority of the 200 homes and businesses were rebuilt in a little over a year and represent many of the buildings still standing in Park City's Old Town today.

Park City continued to boom until the Bankers Panic of 1907. The Panic, along with the lack of silver demand after World War I, and the Great Depression, brought about the decline of mining in Park City. By the end of the 1950's, what was once the largest silver mining camp in the world was virtually a ghost town.

In an attempt to revive the local economy, the last surviving mining company in Park City applied for a federal loan to start Treasure Mountain Resort. With the help of $1.2 million dollars in federal funds designated by Congress to help depressed rural towns, Treasure Mountain Resort opened in 1963 on approximately 10,000 acres of former mining claims.

The coming of the ski industry breathed much needed life back into the local economy and Park City was able to recover from the decline of the mining industry. Since that time, Park City has gone on to host events at the 2002 Winter Olympic Games, and is home to three world-class destination resorts including Deer Valley, Park City Mountain Resort, and The Canyons Resort.

Ontario Mill

The Ontario Mill was built in 1877. It consisted of 40 stamps for the crushing of ore, and was the largest and most modern mill in the United States at the time. The mill was located on a hillside at the mouth of Empire Canyon to move ore through the mill more efficiently with the benefit of gravity. The Great Depression spelled the demise of the Ontario Mill and it was demolished in 1924 with the exception of the largest smokestack, which continued to tower over Park City until 1949.

Ontario Mill, circa 1881.

The Ontario Mill Site barely warrants cursory glance as travelers drive up Utah Highway 224 to Silver Lake at Deer Valley and the luxurious developments in Empire Pass. The mill site is bisected by a dirt access road, as well as a runaway truck ramp for large vehicles coming down canyon. For the curious, closer inspection reveals remnants of the mill foundations and other artifacts from the dismantled mill.

Above: Ore car tracks, Highway 224, 2010.
Left: Looking southwest across the former Ontario Mill Site. Daly Bowl in the background.

Daly West Mine

The Daly West Mine was established by John Daly in 1881. Hoisting equipment was installed and a 1500 foot deep shaft was sunk. The mine proved to be one of the richest in the Park City Mining District. On July 15th, 1902, the deadliest mining incident in Park City mining history occurred when an explosion of an underground supply of dynamite killed 25 miners in the Daly West. Poison gas created by the explosion traveled underground to the Ontario Mine, killing nine miners there. The tragedy prompted the adoption of a state law banning the underground storage of large explosive caches.

Daly West Mine, circa 1896.

Montage Deer Valley

The Daly West Mine site is now the home of the Montage Deer Valley. Conscious of the area's rich mining history, the Montage made a dedicated effort to preserve the site's mining structures and relics, including the Daly West head frame and several outbuildings. The three contemporary photographs shown here demonstrate the constant change that takes place in a community. The images to the left were photographed in June 2010, while the image below illustrates the changes that took place between June and November 2010. Opening in December 2010, the Montage Deer Valley features over 200 rooms and suites along with three restaurants and the 35,000 square foot Spa Montage Deer Valley. The 16-acre forested property is pursuing LEED certification and has numerous "green" features designed to minimize its overall carbon footprint.

Preserved Daly West head frame and storage buildings, 2010.

Above: Nearly completed Hotel Montage, November 2010.
Left: Under construction Hotel Montage, June 2010.

Marsac Mill

The Marsac Mill was built in 1874 at the lower end of Swede Alley and featured 20 stamps for processing ore from the Flagstaff Mine. The process of stamping ore consists of crushing the ore with huge weights in order for the silver to be filtered out. With 20 stamps operating, the mill could process 60-70 tons of ore per day. Due to the distance of the Flagstaff Mine and the technical problems associated with Marsac's primitive and poorly designed stamp machinery, the Marsac was one of the least productive mills in the Park City area. In 1904 the mill was torn down. After laying vacant for many years, the Marsac Mill site was transformed into the state-of-the-art Park City Transit Center, which was constructed for the 2002 Winter Olympic Games and continues to serve the Park City community to this day.

Marsac Mill, circa 1890's.

Park City Transit Center, 2010.

Photographer's note: The former Marsac Mill site was one of the most difficult photographs to recreate for this book. The historical image was photographed from a place where a building now stands. To gain the proper perspective on the site, the image of the Park City Transit Center above was photographed from the B.P.O.E building's fire escape, requiring some interesting tripod acrobatics.

Silver King Consolidated Mill

The Silver King Consolidated Mill & lower tram terminal was constructed in the early 1900's by the Grasselli Chemical Company of Cleveland, Ohio for the concentrating of zinc. The four-story building was purchased in 1914 by the Park City Milling Company, which renovated the plant into a chlorination mill for the refining of silver from low-grade ores containing a combination of silver, copper, and lead. The mill was located north of the Union Pacific Depot at the foot of Masonic Hill and processed ore from the King Con Mine and other nearby mines.

The exact location of the former Silver King Consolidated Mill site is difficult to discern, since only a few photographs of the mill survive and none of the photographs have any definitive landmarks outside of the base of Masonic Hill. The contemporary image to the right, was photographed looking northeast from City Park towards the junction of Deer Valley Drive and Bonanza Drive.

Silver King Consolidated Mill & lower tramway terminal, circa 1920's.

City Park, near the junction of Deer Valley Drive & Bonanza Drive, 2010.

California - Comstock Mill, circa early 1900's.

California - Comstock Mill & Thaynes Canyon, 2005.

California - Comstock Mill

The California - Comstock Mill is located near the head of Thaynes Canyon at Park City Mountain Resort, and was constructed around 1900 to process ore from the Comstock Mine. In 1903, the Comstock Mine merged with its rival the California Mine to the south. The California - Comstock was purchased in 1918 by the King Con Mine, and later changed hands to Silver King Consolidated in 1924. In its heyday, the California - Comstock Mill could process 150 tons of ore per day, with a workforce of only four men.

Today, only a portion of the mill building remains, representing the ore house and the crushing jigs structure. The mill is currently in an advanced state of decay and will one day fade into memory.

California - Comstock Mill remnants, autumn 2004.

Silver King Coalition Mines Building

The Silver King Coalition Mines lower terminal building was constructed in 1901, along with the Silver King Aerial Tramway. The tramway transported processed ore from the Silver King Mill in Woodside Gulch, down to the Silver King Coalition Mines building, where it was loaded onto railcars for distribution to outside markets. Miners and coal were also transported back uphill to the mine. The aerial tramway saved money and replaced the slow and dangerous horse wagons carrying heavy ore down steep canyons. Located at the terminus to the Denver & Rio Grande Railroad's Parley's Canyon Line, the facility operated until 1952.

Several prominent Utah figures made their fortunes as investors in the Silver King Coalition Mines Company. The investors included David Keith and Thomas Kearns, who purchased the Salt Lake Tribune newspaper in 1901. David Keith became president of the Salt Lake Tribune newspaper, while Thomas Kearns was elected a U.S. Senator that same year. Other famous investors included John Judge and Susannah Bransford Emery, who was known internationally as Utah's Silver Queen. Susannah Bransford Emery reportedly made $1,000 a day from her interest in the Silver King Mine in 1894.

Silver King Coalition Building, circa 1922.

The Silver King Coalition Mines building met its demise in 1981 when it burned to the ground. The nearly all-wooden structure burned so intensely that the heat from the fire melted the painted sign of the Sinclair garage across Park Avenue, exposing the old National Garage sign beneath. The fire was started by three boys after a Beach Boys concert, who were later arrested. However the fire started, a great iconic Park City landmark was lost.

The former Silver King Coalition Mines building site is now home to Park City Mountain Resort's Town Lift, as well as the Caledonian Building and Town Lift Plaza. The only physical reminders of the Silver King Coalition Building are the remaining tramway towers that parallel the Town Lift west of Old Town.

Above: Silver King Aerial Tramway towers parallel the Town Lift up Treasure Hill, 2004.
Left: Park Avenue and the former Silver King Coalition Mines building site, 2010.

Silver King Mill

Located at the head of Woodside Gulch, the original Silver King Mill was built in 1901 to process ore from the Silver King Mine. The Silver King Mine was the crown jewel of the Silver King Coalition Mine Company, and boasted three boarding houses, an assay office, a machine shop, superintendent's house, and an aerial tramway loading station. After the original 1898 structure burned, the mill was rebuilt in 1921 and operated until 1945.

Silver King Mill, circa 1935.

Silver King Mill, 2010.

The historic setting of the Silver King Mill has changed considerably over the years. The dense complex of transfer buildings and boarding houses have been dismantled or moved. The construction of Treasure Mountain Resort, eventually becoming what is now known as Park City Mountain Resort today, also altered the setting. The contemporary image above features the original Treasure Mountain gondola angle-station building in the left center, as well as the juxtaposition of the modern Crescent Lift on Crescent Ridge above.

Of all the historic mills in the Park City area, the Silver King is the most intact and offers the best sense of what an operating stamp mill was like in the mining heyday of bygone years. Many relics and artifacts litter the mill site, while the foundation provides wildlife habitat for several families of marmots.

Interior Silver King Mill, 2010.

Marmot, mill foundation, 2010.

Daly Judge Mill

The Daly Judge Mine & Mill was originally constructed in the early 1900's. The complex included the mill, machine shop, ore trestle, bunk house, superintendent's house, and associated storage buildings. The mill operated until 1931 and was later put up for auction in 1943 and dismantled for scrap.

Despite significant alterations and grading to the original mill site for flood control and city water development, many mining remnants such as original foundations and mining-era artifacts can be found.

Built in 1925 the Daly Judge Mill aerial tramway delivered processed ore to a loading station at the lower end of Empire Canyon. Today only eight towers remain along the steep hillsides of Empire Canyon as a testament to the once extensive infrastructure of Park City's mining era.

Daly Judge Mill, circa 1920's.

Looking north down Daly Canyon across the former Daly Judge Mill site, 2010.

Daly Judge Mill, foundation remnants, 2009.

Daly Judge Mine & Mill Aerial Tramway & Tailings, Empire Canyon, 2010.

Judge Mine Assay Office

The Judge Mine Assay Office building was constructed in 1920. The concrete building consists of an assay office in front and a much larger section in back which was utilized as a change room for miners and mill workers.

The Judge Mine Assay Office building is one of the few remaining structures from the vast Daly Judge Mine and Mill complex that once occupied Empire Canyon. The few structures that remain include the Assay Office, the Explosives Bunker, and several additional structures to the west associated with the Alliance Mine.

Judge Mine Assay Office, circa 1920's.

Judge Mine Assay Office, spring 2010.

Explosives Bunker near Judge Mine Assay Office, 2010.

Alliance Boarding House, 2009.

Judge Zinc Smelter

The Judge Electrolytic Zinc Smelter operated from 1914 to 1919. The mill processed zinc which occurs naturally in Park City's lead and silver ores. Zinc was stockpiled by John Judge and other mine owners to process and sell when zinc prices were high. The mill stood on what is now the corner of Deer Valley Drive and Royal Street.

Judge Zinc Smelter, circa 1917.

As with many historic sites in the Park City area, the former Judge Electrolytic Zinc Smelter site at the corner of Deer Valley Drive and Royal Street goes largely unnoticed by passing motorists. The area surrounding the site is now home to some of the most valuable real estate in Utah.

Judge Electrolytic Zinc Mill site, 2010.

Park City Consolidated Mine

The Park Con Mine, as it was called by local miners, was founded in 1928. Between 1929 and 1939, the Park Con produced nearly $4,000,000 in metals. Like many local mines, the Park Con suffered from the general decline of metal prices during the Great Depression and eventually closed in the late 1940's.

Park City Consolidated Mine, circa 1930's.

Entrance St. Regis Deer Valley, 2010.

St. Regis Deer Valley

The St. Regis Deer Valley opened on the former Park City Consolidated Mine site in November 2009. Featuring 181 guest rooms and suites, the St. Regis Deer Valley's architectural design utilizes the natural terrain, whereby guests are whisked by funicular from the lower resort Porte Cochere to the main lodge situated on the ridge above. Other amenities at the St. Regis Deer Valley include the St. Regis Athletic Club, J&G Grill, the St. Regis Wine Vault bar, and the 14,000 square-foot Remè de Spa.

St. Regis Deer Valley & Snow Park Lodge, autumn 2010.

Silver King Consolidated - Spiro Machine Shop

The Silver King Consolidated - Spiro Machine Shop building was constructed in 1929. The building was extensively renovated in 2006 during the development of the Silver Star multi-family and commercial project and is now home to the Sundance Institute. Founded by Robert Redford in 1981 to promote and foster independent American film, the Institute's programs include the internationally recognized Sundance Film Festival, held in and around Park City each January.

The Spiro Machine Shop is part of the larger Silver King Consolidated - Spiro Tunnel Complex. The Spiro Tunnel was constructed in 1916 as part of a plan to drain water from the Silver King and Thaynes Canyon mines, which was a common problem in the Park City area. Solon Spiro, who headed the company dynamiting the tunnel, planned on finding valuable ore to assist in the financing of the operation. After finding no valuable ore, the company went bankrupt, and Spiro was forced to sell his mine. Unfortunately for Spiro, the new owners stuck a significant ore vein just 40 feet further. The Spiro Tunnel continues to provide water for Park City to this day.

Above: Spiro Machine Shop, circa 1940's.
Left: Spiro Mine Tunnel, 2009.

Sundance Institute

Silver Star is also home to the Spiro Arts, an artist-in-residence community and workshop center, which is housed in the former Silver King Consolidated Sawmill Building. Spiro Arts is home to an eclectic community of visual and literary artists. The center also hosts open studio events, a public lecture series, Writers at Work Conference, Art Auction Gala, as well as summer workshops for adults and children.

Above: Egyptian Theatre, Sundance Film Festival, 2011.
Left: Silver King Consolidated Sawmill Building, 2003.

Sundance Institute at the Silver Star, 2010.

Architecture of Old Town: If These Walls Could Talk

Looking south up Main Street at the turn of the century. Photographed after the Great Fire of 1898, this image illustrates the rebuilding that took place in a short time span. On the left side of the photograph, one can see Historic City Hall, as well as the construction of the original fire alarm bell tower.

Main Street, circa 1901.

Looking south up Main Street today, the architecture along this block still features many of the historic buildings and storefronts from the mining heyday of the early 1900's. Along the left you will notice the Historic City Hall, built in 1884 and rebuilt after being damaged in the Great Fire of 1898. Also prominent is the "10 o'clock whistle" tower, which was originally built in 1901 as a fire alarm bell tower with the reconstruction of the Historic City Hall. Later, the bell was removed and replaced with an electric siren. The siren was tested every night at 10 p.m. to assure its operation in an emergency. The siren became known as the "10 o'clock whistle", and was used as a curfew signal by some parents for the young kids of Park City. The whistle still sounds at 10 p.m. to this day.

Above: Main Street, 2010.
Right: Historic storefronts, Main Street, 2010.

Old Town, Park City

Park City looking south towards Old Town. Photographed in 1891, the image depicts the mining boomtown heyday with three operating mills visible. From the left to right: Crescent Mill at the far left, Marsac Mill, and the Ontario Mill in the background just left of center.

Old Town Park City, circa 1891

Overlook, Old Town Park City, 2010.

Much has changed in Park City during the last century. Recreation and tourism is the primary economic engine, and despite nearly a half billion dollars worth of silver, lead, zinc, and other valuable minerals being taken from the ground, the Park City area has not had an operating mine since the early 1980's. All of the old turn of the century mills, which were once models of mining technology, are now all gone save the Silver King Mill in Woodside Gulch. Lodges, condominium projects, commercial buildings, and renovated historic residences now dominate the skyline of Old Town Park City.

Star Meat and Grocery

The Star Meat & Grocery building was built in 1898 shortly after the Great Fire as the Smith & Brim Meat Market. When the original owner George Smith died, his employee George Hoover purchased the business and renamed the market Star Meat & Grocery. The market operated until the 1950's.

Star Meat and Grocery, circa 1920's.

Talisker on Main

The former Star Meat & Grocery sat vacant until 1963, when an antique store opened and operated until the early 1980's. The popular folk art gallery Queen of Arts occupied the building from 1982 to 2005.

Presently, the building that started as a meat market over 100 years ago is the Talisker on Main restaurant, which features a fusion of the various menus from Talisker's private clubhouses. Under the culinary direction of Chef John Murcko, Talisker on Main enables the public to experience Talisker Club cuisine, service, and ambiance in one venue. Talisker is the developer of the Park City area communities of Tuhaye, Empire Pass, and Red Cloud, which is located near the seminal Flagstaff Mine.

Talisker on Main, 2010.

Interior, Talisker on Main, 2010.

Windsor Billiards

The Mission style building that stands at 447 Main Street in Old Town Park City has a storied past and has featured many iconic occupants. Built in 1905, the building has housed the Utah Independent Telephone Company, the Utah Power & Light Company offices, a liquor store, various saloons, and a bowling alley.

Windsor Billiards, 1927.

No Name Saloon

The venerable building at 447 Main is now home to the No Name Saloon, which is a local favorite with locals and tourists alike. Pictured from left to right are the employees and owners: Nicole Ruesch, Marco Peretti, Ronnie Wedig, Frank Dwyer, Jessie Schetler, and Stephanie Frisk.

Interior, No Name Saloon, 2010.

No Name Saloon, 2010.

Golden Rule Mercantile

The Golden Rule Mercantile building was built in 1909, and features a common design for a commercial store front at the turn of the century. The building has housed various stores over the years including the J.C. Penney Company's Golden Rule Mercantile variety store, Day's Market, and Safeway.

The Golden Rule Mercantile, 1927.

350 Main, 2010.

350 Main New American Brasserie

The former Golden Rule Mercantile building is now home to 350 Main New American Brasserie restaurant, which has meticulously renovated the building while preserving the original tin tiled ceiling on the main floor. Featuring the cuisine of Chef Michael Le Clerc, 350 Main is a favorite locals restaurant.

Interior, 350 Main, 2010.

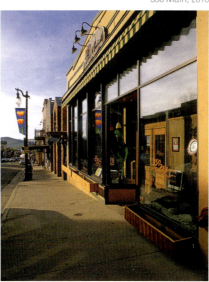

350 Main, 2010.

First National Bank

The First National Bank was constructed in 1898 and in addition to First National Bank, the building also served as the offices of the Silver King Coalition Mining Company, among others over the years.

Above: First National Bank, 1927.
Left: Interior, First National Bank, 1927.

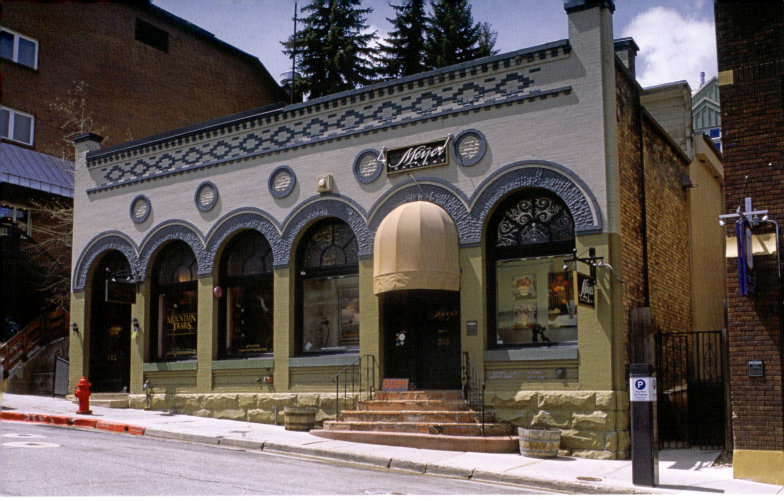

Meyer Gallery

The First National Bank building is now home to the Meyer Gallery and Mountain Trails Gallery. The exterior of the building still retains its historic Victorian commercial style, as well as the original bank vault, which is located in the Meyer Gallery.

Above: First National Bank Building, 2010.
Right: Bank Vault, First National Bank Building, 2010.

The New York Cafe - Bandits Grill & Bar

The building at 440 Main Street is a typical commercial structure from Park City's early mining days. Over the years the building has housed the New York Café, the Park City Variety Store, Texas Reds, and is now home to Bandits' Grill & Bar.

Above: The New York Café, circa 1930's.
Right: Bandits' Grill & Bar, 2010.

China Bridge

During the early boom years of Park City, many Chinese laborers migrated to the town after the completion of the local rail lines into town. In the late 1880's, approximately 300 Chinese settled in the area that is now Swede Alley and built tin-roofed shacks. In order to walk to Main Street, the residents of Rossi Hill had to travel through the area, which they resented. Thus, in 1888 a bridge was constructed over Chinatown. The original was damaged in the fire of 1898 and a new bridge was constructed in 1915, which stood until 1954.

Today the site of the old China Bridge is occupied by the China Bridge Parking structure. A newer stairway still ascends Rossi Hill from the China Bridge site utilizing the original routing. The vacant store fronts seen in the historic photograph are now home to Java Cow Café & Bakery and Chimayo restaurant.

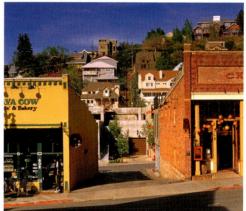

Above: China Bridge site, 2010.
Left: China Bridge, circa 1940's.

Morrison - Merrill & Co.

The Morrison - Merrill & Co. building and lumberyard were constructed in 1925. The gabled roof and false front were popular architectural elements for this time period. Morrison - Merrill operated out of the location until 1948, when Utah Coal & Supply Company relocated from across the street and changed its name to Utah Coal & Lumber. The building was sold in 1976 and converted by the new owners into the Utah Coal & Lumber Restaurant.

Morrison - Merrill & Co. building, circa 1920's.

Easy Street - The Sky Lodge

After the closing of the Utah Coal & Lumber Restaurant, White Pine Touring occupied the building for five years in the late 1990's. Easy Street Brasserie & Bar opened in 2002 after an extensive renovation of the original Morrison - Merrill & Co. building. However, as seen below in 2004, the original Morrison - Merrill & Co. site had not changed much over the years.

Just a few short years later, the former lumberyard site changed dramatically with the construction of The Sky Lodge in 2007. From lumberyard to luxury accommodations, the adaptive reuse of the original Morrison - Merrill & Co. building site illustrates the constant stream of change within the Park City community.

Easy Street Brasserie & Bar, 2004.

Above: The Sky Lodge entrance, 2010.
Left: Easy Street Brasserie, 2010.

Kimball's Garage

Kimball's Garage was constructed in 1929 on the original site of the Kimball Brothers Livery. The livery was an integral provider of transportation during Park City's early mining boom. During the 1910's & 1920's primary transportation shifted from horse to automobile. The Kimball's Garage building represents a snapshot of that transitory time.

Kimball's Garage, circa 1920's.

Kimball Art Center

In 1976, arts lover Bill Kimball and members of the Park City community renovated the abandoned garage into the non-profit Kimball Arts Center. The Kimball Arts Center was again renovated in preparation for the 2002 Winter Olympic Games, which restored the original brick façade that had been covered in the original arts center renovation. The Kimball Arts Center provides a variety of community oriented art programs, as well as staging the regionally known Park City Kimball Arts Festival each summer.

Kimball Art Center, 2010.

Interior Kimball Art Center, 2010.

The Line

Prostitution was a fact of life for all western turn-of-the-century mining boomtowns, and Park City was no exception. Park City's red light district was a line of small houses along what is now Deer Valley Drive, and was referred to by locals as "The Line." With a string of brothels and nearly 30 saloons operating at the turn of the century, Park City soon earned the nickname "Sin City" in other parts of Utah.

Today, most of the original structures that lined what is now Deer Valley Drive are gone. A few remnants remain along with the newly constructed Line Condominiums, named in homage to Park City's colorful heritage.

"The Line" Red Light District, circa early 1900's

Above: Remnants Deer Valley Drive, 2005.
Right: Deer Valley Drive, 2010.

New Park Hotel, circa 1920's.

New Park Hotel

The New Park Hotel was built in 1913 on the site of the former Park City Hotel, which burned down in 1912. The hotel was owned and operated by Mrs. Marie Hethke O'Keefe and was a popular stopping place for travelers passing through Park City. Mrs. O'Keefe operated the New Park Hotel until it closed in 1952. The hotel lay vacant for over a decade, until an effort was made to renovate and modernized the hotel in the mid-1960's. The newly renovated hotel was known as The Claimjumper, and featured the Claimjumper Steakhouse, quickly becoming a favorite among locals and tourists. After 30 years of operation, the owners of the Claimjumper Hotel sold the building to outside developers during the real estate boom of the early 2000's. As of 2010, the building remains vacant with plans to renovate the building yet again on hold due to poor economic conditions.

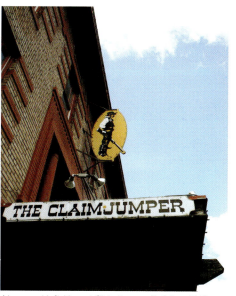

Above and left: Vacant Claimjumper Building, 2010.

Park Motor - National Garage

The National Garage was originally built as the Beggs & Buckley livery stable in 1904 to service the workhorses that pulled heavy ore carts up and down to the mines. As the automobile became the primary mode of transportation in Park City, the owners of the livery began to service cars and changed the name to Beggs & Buckley Garage. The name of the garage was later changed to the National Garage and then finally Sinclair Park Motor. The garage operated until 1942.

Park Motor, circa 1950's.

National Garage & High West Distillery

After being used as storage for many years, the National Garage was sold in 1997 to Park City Municipal Corporation in an effort to prevent the building's demolition. Looking for a unique property to house Utah's first whiskey distillery since Prohibition, the owners of the High West Distillery purchased the property from Park City Municipal Corporation in 2007, with a plan to assure for the historic preservation of the National Garage and adjacent Beggs Home. The meticulous historic renovation provided room for High West's distillery operations, a restaurant, tasting room, and saloon. The Utah Heritage Foundation presented High West Distillery with their 2010 Heritage Award for the Adaptive Reuse of the Beggs Home and National Garage.

National Garage - High West Distillery, 2010.

National Garage - High West Distillery, 2010.

Distillery Interior, 2010.

Union Pacific Railroad Depot

The Union Pacific Railroad Depot was built in 1886, five years after the Union Pacific line came to Park City in 1881. The Union Pacific Spur Line transported much needed coal to the silver mines and carried ore to outside markets to be smelted. The depot served as the home of the station agent until 1976, when the agency was closed. Few trains traveled into Park City after that time, with the notable exceptions being lumber deliveries and the occasional ski passenger trains. In 1986 the final train ran on the Park City line. Afterwards, the rail line went into disuse and was eventually sold to the state of Utah, which converted it into the Union Pacific Rail Trail.

Union Pacific Railroad Depot, early 1900's.

Zoom

The depot sat virtually unused and was damaged by fire in 1985. The depot was eventually sold to a private party who converted the historic building into a restaurant. In 1995 the restaurant Zoom opened and features many historic touches including an original scale for weighing train freight in the main dining room.

Zoom, 2010.

Zoom, 2010.

Denver & Rio Grande Railroad Depot

The Denver & Rio Grande line was originally built as a narrow gauge rail line by the Salt Lake & Eastern Railway in 1890, in an effort to break Union Pacific's coal monopoly. After gaining the rights to the rail line in 1898, the Denver & Rio Grande Railroad improved and expanded the rail line to a standard gauge and built a depot for the handling of freight and passengers. The Denver & Rio Grande line was abandoned in 1946, at which time most of the line was dismantled and abandoned.

Denver & Rio Grande Railroad Depot & Park Avenue, 1920's.

The last remaining vestige of the Denver & Rio Grande Depot is the depot's original baggage shed. The historical context of the original depot site was significantly altered with the development of the Town Lift Plaza in the early 1990's. The depot's baggage shed was most recently used as a bank building, but currently sits vacant.

Rio Grande Railroad Depot Remnant & Park Avenue, 2009.

Crescent Railroad

In 1884, the Crescent Mine Company built a narrow gauge railway to haul ore from their mine in Thaynes Canyon down to the Crescent Mill in Old Town. With the completion of the tramway, the Crescent Mine owners were able to transport their ore more efficiently than the standard horse and mule ore wagons. However, the new railway wasn't without its own problems. In the summer of 1885, caterpillars made the rails slippery enough to make braking impossible, causing the wreck of a load of down bound ore cars.

Above: Crescent Train pulling ore carts back up grade, 1885.
Left: Abandoned Crescent Railroad Grade, early 1900's.

Former Crescent Railroad Grade, 2010.

As silver prices fluctuated during the 1890's the Crescent Mine and associated railway operated intermittently. Eventually, the mine closed and the rails were pulled up in 1900. Today, the former Crescent Railroad grade continues to run northwest from Lowell Avenue and is now a paved private drive on its lower stretches.

Park City Fire Department

The Park City Fire Department was organized in 1884 by the newly formed city council to meet the growing demands of a booming community. The fire department was originally housed in the Historic City Hall on Main Street, affording the firemen the ability to respond in a moments' notice.

Firemen in front of Historic City Hall, circa 1920's.

Historic City Hall – Park City Museum

Members of the Park City Fire Department outside Historic City Hall and the Park City Museum. From left to right: Assistant Chief Bob Zanetti, Engineer Ryan Christensen, Fire Fighter Neil Enquist, Paramedic Ron Palmer Leger, and Captian Brent Thompson. One of the Park City Fire Department's original 1926 Dodge fire trucks has returned to its former garage inside the fire alarm bell tower, which was part of the Park City Museum's recent nine million dollar renovation.

Park City Fire Department, Historic City Hall and the Park City Museum, 2010.

Park City Museum Interior, 2010.

Original 1926 Graham Brothers Dodge Fire Truck, 2010.

Park City Territorial Jail, 2010.

Sheriff's Office

The Summit County Sheriff's Office building was built in 1905. Because the Sheriff wasn't based in Park City, the building was given to Park City in the late 1960's. Since that time the building has been used as the Chamber of Commerce, among other uses. After being vacant for several years the building was sold into private hands and is now home to Prospect, a footwear and accessories retailer.

Summit County Sheriff's Office, 1930's.

Park City Police Department

Park City Police Captain Wade Carpenter and Mayor Dana Williams recreate one of Park City's most iconic historic photographs. Chief Carpenter's dog Hadji patiently poses on one of the Park City Police Department's Harley Davidson motorcycles. Park City has been using Harley Davidson motorcycles longer than any other law enforcement agency in America.

Former Summit County Sheriff's Office, 2010.

Washington School

The Washington School was built in 1889 as part of an effort to respond to the increasing school enrollment associated with Park City's population boom of the late 1880's. Other schools built at the time were the Jefferson School in 1887, and the Lincoln School in 1896.

Built of hammered limestone quarried at Peoa, Utah, the Washington School was one of the few structures in the area to survive the Great Fire of 1898. The school served Park City's educational needs until 1931, when it was closed due to declining enrollments. The building was purchased by the Veterans of Foreign Wars for $200 in 1936, which was well below the original cost of $13,000. The V.F.W. used the facility until the 1950's.

The Washington School sat vacant until the early 1980's, when new owners embarked on an extensive renovation, which included gutting the structure down to its stone walls and rebuilding the interior from the ground up. The Washington School Inn still retains much of the historic charm of the original school house.

Above: Washington Public School, early 1900's.
Right: Washington School Inn, 2010.

Marsac School

Built in 1936, the Marsac School was one of many Public Works buildings constructed in Utah under the New Deal's depression era public works programs. The school was built to consolidate Park City's student population. The Marsac building possesses Public Works Administration Moderne style architecture, with the most prominent examples being the terra cotta coping and the decorative flame motif seen in the parapet elements and the brick pilasters, as well as the concrete staircase. The building sits upon a portion of the former Marsac Mill site, from which is it named. Remnants of the mill's foundation can be seen crossing diagonally along the hillside below the facility in both the historic and contemporary images.

The Marsac School served the educational needs of Park City until 1979. Park City Municipal Corporation purchased and renovated the vacant building in 1983 to consolidate the city's various departments and to maintain a presence in historic Old Town. After housing the Park City Municipal Offices for 25 years, the Marsac building was again renovated in 2009 at a cost of seven million dollars, receiving seismic upgrades, energy efficient technologies, and an extensive interior remodel.

Above: Marsac School, early 1940's
Left: Park City Municipal Building, 2010.

Park City High School

The Park City High School was built in 1926 at a cost of nearly $200,000. The school served Park City high school students for almost fifty years.

Park City High School, circa 1930's.

Former Park City High School, 2010.

Park City Library & Education Center

After outgrowing the library at the former Miner's Hospital, the Park City Library Board commissioned the $2.5 million dollar renovation of the vacant Park City High School in 1993. The building's historic architecture was preserved, while the old gymnasium was converted into a 17,000 square foot library on two levels. The remaining space is filled by various education related activities including the Sundance Film Festival in the Jim Santy Auditorium, the Park City Film Series, and other community events.

U.S. Post Office

The United States Post Office was built on Main Street in 1921. The historic Park City Bandstand can be seen in the background to the left.

Under construction U.S. Post Office, 1921.

Incorporating the original structure from 1921 on the north side of the building, the Park City post office was expanded and renovated in the 1960's and again in 1975. There have been recent talks between Park City Municipal Corporation and the U.S. Postal Service on restoring the Post Office to its original size, and using the remaining space as a park.

Park City U.S. Post Office, 2010.

Park City U.S. Post Office, 2010

St. Mary's Church

The St. Mary's of the Assumption Church was built in 1884, after the original wood church burned down. Made of locally quarried stone, the church is perched atop Park Avenue and continues to serve the local parish to this day.

In 1997, the St. Mary's Parish built a new church in the Snyderville Basin on land donated by Jim and Sally Ivers.

St. Mary's of the Assumption Catholic Church, circa early 1950's

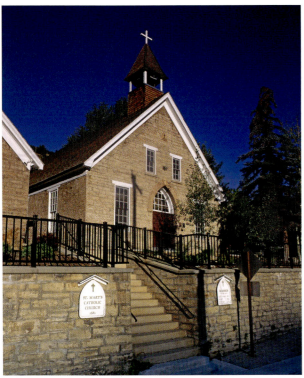

Above: St. Mary's of the Assumption Catholic Church, 2008
Right: St. Mary's Church, Snyderville Basin, 2007

LDS Meeting House

The Park City LDS Meeting House was originally constructed in 1897. However, the original church burned down during the Great Fire of 1898. The structure seen today was built in 1899, along with an addition in 1926. The building served as a meeting house until 1962. After laying vacant for many years, the old meeting house was renovated into The Blue Church Lodge in the late 1970's.

Above: Church of Jesus Christ of Latter Day Saints Meeting House, circa 1920's. Below: The Blue Church Lodge, 2010.

Miners Hospital

The Miners Hospital was built in 1904 for the cost of $5,000, which was raised by local community leaders and the Local No. 144 of the Western Federation of Miners. Situated on the Nelson Farm outside of Old Town, the construction of the hospital enabled miners to seek care without the hardship of the 60-mile round trip to Salt Lake City.

Miners Hospital, circa early 1900's.

Miners Hospital, 2004.

The Miners Hospital served the local community until the late 1950's. After closing, the facility was renovated into a youth hostel for the new Treasure Mountain Resort in the early 1960's. In the late 1970's, redevelopment of the base of Park City Mountain Resort threatened the structure with demolition. Faced with the loss of a local landmark, concerned citizens were able to rally for its preservation. The hospital was moved to its present day location at City Park in 1982, and converted into a library. Today Parkites have a new state-of-the-art medical center at Quinn's Junction.

New IHC Park City Medical Center, 2010.

Skiing in Park City: A Brief History

Skiing in Park City started with miners checking phone lines on skis as early as the 1880's. By 1900, miners were regularly seen traveling to and from the mines on skis that they called "flip flops". Some local miners were even known to catch the mine train uphill to ski back down. In the 1930's, the legendary Alf Engen began organizing ski jump competitions on the tailings piles of the abandoned Creole Mine on Treasure Hill above Old Town. The success of the Creole Mine Jump led to a search for more challenging terrain, and the establishment of the Ecker Hill Ski Jump outside Park City. Completed in 1930, Ecker Hill became one of the premier ski jumps in the world at the time, with many National Meets held at the hill in the 1930's and 1940's. Several world jumping records were broken on Ecker Hill by Alf Engen, and the publicity that the hill garnered helped establish Utah as a ski destination. Ecker Hill's prominence in the jumping world declined in the 1950's as larger and more modern ski jumps were built worldwide, and downhill skiing became more popular as a winter sport.

With the popularity of downhill skiing increasing in the late 1940's, the era of lift served skiing came to Park City with local ski enthusiasts Otto Carpenter and Bob Burns building a ski lift and a warming hut on the site of what is now Deer Valley Resort. Named Snow Park Resort, after a local ski club, the resort operated on weekends and holidays until its closing in 1969. Other resort openings followed with Gorgoza opening a single chair lift near Parley's Summit in 1954, Treasure Mountain Resort in 1963, Park City West in 1968, and Deer Valley Resort in 1981, on the former Snow Park Resort site.

Over the years, Park City's three resorts changed names and ownership. Park City West had the most ownership and name changes, becoming just ParkWest in 1975, Wolf Mountain in 1995, and The Canyons in 1997. Treasure Mountain became Park City Mountain Resort, while Deer Valley has retained the same name and owners since its opening. Through all the changes, Park City's three ski resorts have modernized and expanded to become world-class destinations. The close proximity of several world-class ski resorts to each other, along with the construction of the Utah Winter Sports Park at Bear Hollow in 1993, helped Utah win the bid to host the 2002 Winter Olympic Games in 1995. After the successful conclusion of the 2002 Games, Park City and Utah's ski industry as a whole benefited from the world-wide attention the games provided.

Ecker Hill, circa 1930's.

Ecker Hill, 2010.

Ecker Hill - Utah Olympic Park

After hosting the U.S. National Ski Jumping Championship in 1949, Ecker Hill experienced declining usage throughout the 1950's and was rarely used after 1960. The ski jump was eventually abandoned. Ecker Hill is now preserved as a park in the Pinebrook subdivision, with a few remaining remnants for the curious.

The Utah Winter Sports Park at Bear Hollow was built in 1993 in an attempt to bolster Salt Lake City's bid to host the 2002 Winter Olympic Games. After securing the bid, the facility's name was changed to the Utah Olympic Park and underwent a series of upgrades and renovations in preparation for the Olympic Games. Upgrades included the construction of the $10 million Joe Quinney Winter Sports Center and Alf Engen Ski Museum, which was completed in the fall of 2001 and served as the media center for the world's journalists covering the games. The Utah Olympic Park hosted all of the ski jumping, nordic combined, bobsled, luge, and skeleton events during the 2002 Olympic Games, and currently provides year-round training facilities to develop athletes in winter sports through competition, training and recreational programs.

Utah Olympic Park, 2007.

Nelson Farm

John Nelson settled his family at the base of what is now Park City Mountain Resort, after serving in America's Civil War. Nelson was a farmer and prospector, and discovered many valuable claims in the Park City area. The Miners Hospital was built at the Nelson Farm in 1904, on land donated by the Nelson family.

Nelson Farm, circa early 1920's.

Park City Mountain Resort base area, 2010.

Park City Mountain Resort

Treasure Mountain Resort opened in 1963 as part of an effort by community leaders and the area's last surviving mining company to revive Park City's economy, which was suffering from the long decline in metal prices and the closing of the majority of Park City's mines. With the help of $1.2 million dollars in federal funds designated by Congress to help depressed rural towns, Treasure Mountain Resort opened with a gondola, a chair-lift, and two J-bars. Treasure's first year featured $3.50 lift passes. Skier days were 50,000, which exceeded initial expectations. The resort's name was changed to Park City Ski Area in 1967.

In 1970, the ski operations were sold to Edgar Stern's Royal Street Development Company, which later sold the operations to Alpine Meadows of Tahoe in 1974. The resort was sold again to Ian Cumming in 1995 and was renamed Park City Mountain Resort in 1996. The resort hosted several events at the Winter Olympic Games in 2002, including all of the men's and women's snowboard events and Giant Alpine Slalom. Today, Park City Mountain Resort features 16 lifts, 3,300 acres of terrain spread over eight peaks and nine bowls, in addition to the Olympic Superpipe. Since those first 50,000 skiers in 1963, Park City Mountain Resort has grown to the point that the resort currently has an uphill lift capacity of 30,200 skiers per hour, and plans for additional improvements in the future.

Snow Park Resort

Otto Carpenter and Bob Burns opened the Snow Park Resort in 1946 with one lift and a warming hut. The Ottobahn lift, as it was called, consisted of towers built of local timbers constructed by Carpenter, and metal components fabricated by Burns in the Judge Mine machine shop, where he continued to work. The area had been used in the late 1930's as the site of Park City's "Winter Carnival." The resort closed in 1969, when Snow Park's lease expired and it was not renewed by the mine company.

Ottobahn Lift, Snow Park Resort, circa 1950's.

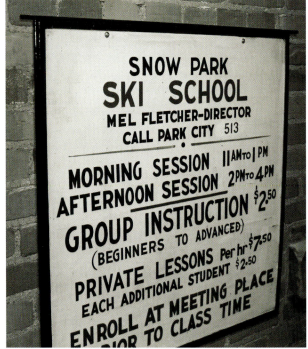

Park City Museum, 2010.

Deer Valley Resort

Deer Valley Resort base area, 2010.

With the opening of Treasure Mountain Resort in 1963, skiing related development began to materialize in Park City. By the 1970's developmental spending increased to the point that the Royal Street Land Company acquired the rights to develop Deer Valley and unveiled a proposal for a six-phase project including not only the original Snow Park, but also Bald Mountain, Flagstaff Mountain, and Empire Canyon. Deer Valley resort opened in December 1981 with five chairlifts, as well as the Snow Park and Silver Lake Lodges. As an homage to the owners of the original Snow Park Resort, two of the chair lifts were named "Burns" and "Carpenter". By the early 1990's, Deer Valley was recognized as one of the elite ski destinations in North America. Today, Deer Valley features 20 lifts and one gondola serving skiing across 6 peaks and over 2,000 acres. Celebrating their 30th anniversary in 2011, Deer Valley was rated the #1 ski resort in North America by SKI Magazine for an unprecedented 4th year in a row.

Park City West

Park City West began operations in 1968, when a lift ticket was $4.50. The resort changed ownership in 1975 and was renamed ParkWest, in order to prevent confusion with Park City Resort. ParkWest was sold in 1995 to a new ownership group, changing the name to Wolf Mountain and became the first resort in Utah to allow snowboarding. In 1997 the resort was sold yet again, this time to American Ski Company, which renamed the resort The Canyons and embarked on a $500 million dollar expansion.

View of Park City West, circa 1974.

The Canyons

From 1997 to 2001, The Canyons expanded from 1,400 acres to 3,500 acres of terrain. The concurrent base area expansion included the construction of the Grand Summit Hotel and Conference Center, as well as the Sundial Lodge. With the expansion complete, The Canyons was the largest resort in Utah and the 5th largest in the United States at the time.

In 2008 The Canyons resort was purchased by Talisker, a privately owned development company based in Toronto, Canada. In 2010, Talisker embarked on a project to recreate the resort, including re-aligning the gondola, installing a state-of-the-art quad-lift with heated seats, adding 300 acres of terrain on Iron Mountain, designing a ski beach at the base, and adding a 20 million gallon snowmaking pond. At the start of the 2010-2011 ski season, The Canyons featured 4,000 acres of terrain, and 19 lifts, spread over 9 peaks and 5 bowls.

Above: Sunrise over St. Mary's Church and The Canyons, 2005.
Left: The Canyons, 2010.

Early Life in the Snyderville Basin

Samuel Snyder arrived in what is now known as the Snyderville Basin in 1850. Along with his nine brothers, Sam Snyder and other early settlers engaged in traditional farming and ranching activities. The labors of these early settlers provided a booming Park City with much needed agricultural products.

Much has changed in the Park City area during the past century. The area has lost the majority of its farms and ranches, due mainly to the escalation of land values making traditional agriculture unprofitable. Park City and the Snyderville Basin are now characterized by resort-related commercial and residential development. In the foreground of the contemporary image to the left, one can see the former Silver King Consolidated - Spiro Tunnel Complex, now transformed into the Silver Star at Park City.

Looking east across the junction of U-224 and U-248, circa 1930's.

View east towards the junction of Hwy. 224 and Kearns Boulevard, 2010.

McPolin Farm

The McPolin barn was built in the 1908 by Dan and Isabelle McPolin utilizing recycled timber salvaged from an old mine tailings pile. Patrick and Grace McPolin inherited the farm in 1923 and operated it as a dairy farm until 1948, when they sold it to the Osguthorpe family. The Osguthorpes operated the barn as a dairy farm until 1990, when Park City purchased the barn along with the surrounding farmland to enhance the city's entry corridor and maintain as open space.

McPolin Farm, circa 1930's.

The McPolin Farm has been extensively refurbished, including the stabilization of the barn and other historic structures, restoration and enhancement of wetlands and stream corridor, and the construction of a hiking/skiing/biking trail through the 160-acre homestead. The McPolin Barn is a favorite of locals and visitors alike, and is the home of many local activities including the annual Scarecrow Festival at the McPolin Farm each fall.

McPolin Farm, 2010.

Left: Farm Ladders, 2005. Right: Scarecrow, 2005.

Pop Jenk's

J.E. Jenkins, aka "Pop Jenks" was a well known local businessman in Park City. Pop Jenk's Lunch near the junction of U-224 and U-248 was a favorite stop for locals and visitors to Park City. Pop Jenks was also an accomplished professional photographer who owned a photography studio on Main Street in Old Town during the 1920's & 1930's. When the Great Depression forced many businesses under, Pop's studio survived by adding a soda fountain and a candy counter.

Pop Jenks avidly captured Park City's history with his Eastman Kodak View Camera. His photographic legacy of several hundred 8"x10" negatives were donated by his daughter Thelma Uriarte to the Park City Historical Society & Museum in 1987. Nearly half of the historical images in *Park City - Past & Present* were photographed by J.E. Jenkins.

Pop Jenk's Lunch burned down and the site later became the home of the Mount Air Café. Over the years the Mount Air Cafe became a favorite breakfast stop for skiers heading into Park City. The Mount Air Café operated for 31 years. In 2006, the son and nephew of the Mount Air Café owners, Jeff Polychronis, along with his business partner Peter Cole, renovated the café into the Squatters Roadhouse Grill & Pub. Squatters is Utah's original brewpub with two other locations in downtown Salt Lake City, and the Salt Lake International Airport.

Above: Pop Jenks, circa 1940's. Below: Squatter's Roadhouse Grill & Pub, 2010.

Above: Kimball Hotel & Ranch, circa 1930's. Below: Kimball Hotel & Ranch, 2010.

Kimball Hotel & Ranch

In the early 1860's William Henry Kimball built the Kimball Hotel and Overland Stage Stop, which became well known by travelers on the old Overland Stage Line. The Pony Express mail route also briefly passed by the ranch. Eventually, the Overland Stage Line was incorporated into the Lincoln Highway. The Lincoln Highway ran from coast to coast and was the precursor to the United States Interstate Highway System. The Kimball Ranch is one of the few remaining operating ranches left in the Snyderville Basin.

Kimball Hotel & Ranch, 2004.

Afterword - A Treasure to Keep?

Like many historic resort towns, Park City faces a fragile balance between tourist related development and historic preservation. Most visitors to Park City expect world-class accommodations along with the historic charm of a turn-of-the-century mining town, and enough open space to provide historical context. Many times development, historic preservation, and open space are diametrically opposed. Today, the most visible of these conflicts in Park City is the community divide over the Treasure Hill project proposed for the lower slopes of Treasure Hill just above Old Town. Proponents of the proposed Treasure project tout the increased tax base, tourism dollars, and open space preserved in the development plan as benefits for Old Town. On the opposite side, opponents believe the project, which was originally approved by the Park City Planning Commission in 1986, will increase traffic on narrow residential streets, glut the rental market with too many rooms, and be a visual eyesore looming above Old Town. Will the proposed Treasure project be a boon to Old Town tourism, or as the proverb states: "kill the goose that laid the golden egg"? Which vision of Park City's future will emerge?

Site Plan for the proposed Treasure Hill project.

Concept rendering for the proposed Treasure Hill project.
Top: Before
Bottom: After

Glenwood Cemetery, 2005.

Miner Statue, Main Street, 2009

Dedication

This book is dedicated to those hearty souls who went before us...the early settlers, miners, farmers, and ranchers. Our life is enriched by their posterity. May we never forget the hardships they endured.

Headstone, Glenwood Cemetery, 2004.

Photography Credits & Notes

Photograph Credits:
Front Cover: Rick Pieros
Back Cover: Park City Museum, Pop Jenks Collection (top) and Rick Pieros (bottom)

Park City Museum:
Daly West Mine 10, Silver King Consolidated Mill (top) 14, California - Comstock Mill (top left) 15, Judge Zinc Smelter 24, Main Street 30, Star Meat & Grocery 34, China Bridge (left) 43, The Line (top) 48, Park Motor - National Garage 50, Crescent Railroad Grade (bottom) 56, Nelson Farm 74, Snow Park Resort (right) 76, Park City West 78, McPolin Farm 82, Kimball Hotel & Ranch (top) 85

Park City Museum, Pop Jenks Collection
Silver King Coalition Building 16, Silver King Mill 18, Daly Judge Mill 20, Judge Mine Assay Office 22, Park City Consolidated Mine 26, Spiro Machine Shop (top) 28, Windsor Billiards 36, The Golden Rule Mercantile 38, First National Bank/Interior 40, The New York Café (left) 42, Morrison & Merrill Co. 44, Kimball's Garage 46, New Park Hotel (top) 49, Denver & Rio Grande Railroad Depot 54, Sheriff's Office 60, Marsac School (top) 63, Park City High School 64, Under construction U.S. Post Office 66, LDS Meeting House (top) 69, Snyderville View 80, Pop Jenks (top) 84

Used by permission, Utah State Historical Society:
Old Town Park City 7 (top), Ontario Mill 8, Marsac Mill 12, Old Town Park City 32, Union Pacific Railroad Depot 52, Crescent Mine Train (top) 56, Firemen - Historic City Hall 58, Washington School (top) 62, St. Mary's Church (top right) 68, Miners Hospital 70, Ecker Hill 72

Rick Pieros Photography:
Overlook, Old Town Park City (title page), Miner's Shack 2, Sunrise St. Mary's 3, McPolin Farm 4, California - Comstock Mill 5, Alaska Boarding House/Welcome Sign 6, Utah Olympic Park (bottom) 7, Ontario Mill Site/Ore Cart Tracks 9, Montage Deer Valley (all) 11, Park City Transit Center 13, City Park 14, California - Comstock Mill (bottom left & right) 15, Park Avenue/Silver King Tramway Towers 17, Silver King Mill/Mill Interior/Marmot 19, Daly Judge Mill site and remnants (all) 21, Judge Mine Assay Office/Explosives Bunker/Alliance Mine Boarding House 23, Judge Zinc Smelter site 25, St. Regis Deer Valley (all) 27, Spiro Tunnel (bottom) 28, Sundance Institute/Sawmill Building/Egyptian Theater 29, Main Street/Historic storefronts 31, Overlook, Old Town Park City 33, Talisker on Main/Interior 35, No Name Saloon/Interior 37, 350 Main (all) 39, Meyer Gallery/Interior 41, Bandits Grill & Bar (right) 42, China Bridge (right) 43, Easy Street - The Sky Lodge (all) 45, Kimball Arts Center/Interior 47, Remnants/Deer Valley Drive (bottom left/bottom right) 48, Claimjumper (bottom left/bottom right) 49, National Garage - High West Distillery (all) 51, Zoom (all) 53, Denver & Rio Grande Railroad Depot & Park Avenue 55, Former Crescent Railroad Grade 57, Historic City Hall - Park City Museum (all) 59, Former Sheriff's Office 61, Washington School Inn (bottom) 62, Park City Municipal Building (bottom) 63, Former Park City High School 65, Park City Post Office (all) 67, St. Mary's Church (left & bottom) 68, The Blue Church Lodge (bottom) 69, Miners Hospital/Park City Medical Center 71, Ecker Hill/Utah Olympic Park 73, Park City Mountain Resort 75, Snow Park Resort Sign (left) 76, Deer Valley Resort 77, Sunrise St. Mary's Church/The Canyons 79, Snyderville View 81, McPolin Farm/Farm Ladders/Scarecrow (all) 83, Squatter's Roadhouse Grill & Pub (bottom) 84, Kimball Hotel & Ranch (bottom) 85, Glenwood Cemetery/Miner Statue/Headstone (all) 87

Used by permission, Treasure Hill project/Mike Sweeney:
Treasure Hill photographic renderings (all) 86

Photography Notes - Rick Pieros:
The photographic work by Rick Pieros represented in *Park City - Past & Present* were captured using traditional film methods. Rick Pieros uses a variety of camera mediums including 35mm and medium format cameras, including Nikon, Canon & Mamyia products using primarily Fuji films. Any "digital darkroom" work is strictly limited to traditional darkroom techniques such as contrast control, color correction, and removal of dust from film surface.

All photographs Copyright © 2011 Rick Pieros Photography unless otherwise noted.

Book design by Riverbed Design, riverbeddesign.com